Sophie

Makes Friends

by **Sarah, Duchess of York**

Illustrated by Ian Cunliffe

Sophie Makes Friends

helping hand books

First published in Great Britain 2007 by Lloyds Pharmacy Ltd
Sapphire Court, Walsgrave Triangle, Coventry CV2 2TX
www.lloydspharmacy.com

In consultation with Cameron Wilson Ltd

Story and illustrations © Copyright Startworks Ltd 2007

'Ten Helpful Hints' © Copyright Lloyds Pharmacy Ltd 2007

All rights reserved

No part of this publication may be reproduced, stored in a retrieval system or transmitted
in any form or by any means, electronic, mechanical, photocopying, recording or otherwise,
without the prior permission of the respective copyright owners.

Illustrated by Ian Cunliffe

'Ten Helpful Hints' contributed by Dr. Richard Woolfson,
child psychologist, Fellow of the British Psychological Society.

Printed in China

British Library Cataloguing in Publication Data
A catalogue record for this book is available from the British Library

ISBN 978-1-906260-11-8

All children face many new experiences as they grow up and helping
them to understand and deal with each is one of the most demanding
and rewarding things we do as parents. The helping hand books are
for both children and parents to read, perhaps together. Each simple
story describes a childhood experience and shows some of the ways
in which to make it a positive one. I do hope these books encourage
children and parents to talk about these sometimes difficult issues;
talking together goes a long way to finding a solution.

Sarah

Sarah, Duchess of York

S ophie liked her new school.
Mrs Andersen, her new teacher, was
very good at making things interesting.

It wasn't so much the classroom, more the free time that Sophie was not so sure about.

Some of the other children in her class seemed to have so many friends and they were always playing together.

Sophie liked them all but she wasn't always included in the games.

So when she was, she did her best to make sure it was her turn.

Coming home from school one day, Sophie's Mum asked her if she had had a nice day.

Normally Sophie would just say 'yes' but she had not been included in the games at all that day and she was upset.

So she said, "Well, no Mummy, not really."

"Why ever was that?" asked her Mum.

"I really wanted to join in the games at break but the others wouldn't let me."

And Sophie burst into tears.

"Sophie," said her Mum gently, "I'm sure there was a reason. Perhaps there were too many playing already."

"But it's not just that," said Sophie, "some of the others seem to have so many friends. And I don't have any."

"That's not true," said her Mum. "There's Charlotte and Poppy and you went to Harry's birthday party the other day."

"But all the others have lots and lots of friends," said Sophie. "I only have one or two and sometimes end up on my own."

7

"But it's not the number of friends you have that is important," said her Mum.

"The important thing is to have friends who care about you, not just who will play with you.

Friendship is a special thing which needs to be looked after if it is to grow.

And friends can start even closer than the school playground," her Mum explained.

"Your little brother wants to be your best friend.
You could care for him a little more."

Sophie felt a little sad about that.
She knew her Mum was right about Joshua, her
little brother.

Starting tomorrow, she would spend more time
with him, even if he did like to pull her hair!

A few days later, Sophie's Mum said to her,

"Why don't we have Charlotte and Poppy round to play at the weekend?"

"I don't think they'll want to," said Sophie gloomily.

"We'll never know unless we ask," said her Mum.

And she was right, the girls were pleased to be asked and were dropped off to spend an afternoon with Sophie.

"Let's play tag," said Poppy.

"I'll be it!" shouted Sophie straight away.

For a little while, they all ran around but soon Poppy and Charlotte had had enough.

"Why do you always have to be it?" said Poppy.

"Yes," said Charlotte, "it's no fun when we don't all have a go."

Just then, Sophie's Dad came along and, seeing the looks on the girls' faces, said,

"I think you've had enough of tag.
I've got a better idea. Why don't we build a den?"

The girls loved this idea and rushed around the garden finding bits of branches and leaves to make the den.

Dad organised the building, first with the big branches to form the outside of the den and then using the smaller branches and the leaves to make the walls.

Before long, they had made a cosy little shelter which the three of them could just squeeze into.

Dad found a piece of old carpet in the garage which fitted perfectly.

"You three look so snug in there, I think you'll want to sleep in there," said Dad.

"Oh can we?" chorused the girls.

"Well you might have to share it with a few mice and spiders," said Dad.

The girls all shrieked and clung on to each other.

Sophie's Mum heard the noise and came out to see what was happening.

"That looks great!" she said.

"I'll bring you some drinks and a snack so that you can cool down after all that hard work."

Sophie's little brother Joshua also came to see what was going on. Sophie rushed to him, gave him a hug and took him to see the den where he watched the three friends, smiling happily.

When Mum brought the drinks, she said,

"It's such a special den, you'll have to give it a name."

The girls thought about that and, after a while, Poppy said, "I suppose it should be 'Sophie's Den'."

"I don't think so," said Sophie, "in fact, definitely not."

"The three of us made it together and the three of us will use it together.

I think it should be called 'Friends Den' because we are good friends, aren't we?"

The three girls looked at each other.

"Friends Den!"

they all said together and laughed.

TEN HELPFUL HINTS
FOR PARENTS TO HELP THEIR CHILDREN
MAKE FRIENDS by Dr. Richard Woolfson

1. Suggest games that require co-operation rather than competition. Playing together is one of the best techniques for teaching children how to be friendly.

2. Show your child how to share and take turns. Don't be impatient when your child complains about sharing but explain to her that the rules benefit her as much as the others, and show that you are pleased when she does share.

3. Praise her when she shows kindness. When you see your child helping a friend, make a big fuss and let her know how pleased you are.

4. Teach compromise. Explain to your child that both her and her friend need to change their ideas in some way so that they both come away from a dispute with a feeling of satisfaction. Give her examples.

5. Allocate 'helping' tasks to your child at home. For instance, ask her to help her younger brother tidy his toys, or perhaps help you set out cutlery on the table.

6. Make sure you set a good example. Make a special effort to be pleasant and supportive with each other, so that your child can copy you in her own friendships.

7. Teach positive body language. Suggest that she has a smile on her face when she meets others, that she makes good eye-contact, that she stands confidently and that she looks interested in what they have to say.

8. Encourage her at home to say what she feels and to encourage others to voice their views as well. Friendships work best when a child is able to express her feelings and ideas using spoken language.

9. Let her know that hitting out is unacceptable. The natural tendency for many children is to raise their hand against anyone who annoys them, so make it clear that she should always resolve a problem through words, not violence. Teach her things to say so that she has an alternative to lashing out.

10. Make friendships happen. While you cannot manufacture a friendship for your child, you can encourage her to be friends with the children you like, for instance, by taking them all on an outing together.

The helping hand books

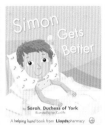

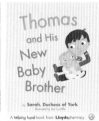

Lloydspharmacy